SNOW WHITE AND THE SEVEN DWARFS

by Margaret and Carson Davidson

illustrated by Yuri Salzman

SCHOLASTIC INC

New York   Toronto   London   Auckland   Sydney

*These tales of magic
and make-believe are
dedicated to Bill Haber,
who has his own
special brand of magic.*

ISBN 0-590-40504-7

Text copyright © 1987 by Margaret and Carson Davidson.
Illustrations copyright © 1987 by Yuri Salzman.
All rights reserved. Published by Scholastic Inc.
MAKE BELIEVE IT'S YOU is a trademark of Scholastic Inc.

12 11 10 9 8 7 6 5 4 3 2 1   7 8 9/8 0 1 2/9

Printed in the U.S.A.   11
First Scholastic printing, March 1987

WAIT! READ THIS FIRST:

Most books are about other people. This book is about *you*. What happens to you depends on what you decide to do. Do you want to meet a dragon? Or a magician? Or a handsome prince? There are many adventures waiting for you in this book.

But there is one thing you must remember. Do not read this book from the first page to the last. If you do, the story won't make sense. Instead, start on page one and read until you come to your first choice. Then turn to the page you decide on and see what happens. Each choice will lead you to another choice — until your adventure comes to an end. Then it is time to go back and start all over again.

HAVE FUN!!

Your name is Snow White. You are a Princess and are very beautiful. Each day you grow more beautiful. And that — *that* is why you are in terrible danger right now.

How did you get in such trouble? Well . . . it was like this. Your mother was the Queen, and a few years ago she died. After a while, your father, the King, married again.

Your new stepmother was the most beautiful woman in all the land. But she was also very proud. She hated the idea that anyone else could be more beautiful than she was.

Every morning she stood in front of a magic mirror that hung in her room and asked:

> *"Mirror, mirror on the wall,*
> *Who is the fairest one of all?"*

And the magic mirror always answered:

> *"You are the fairest one of all."*

Until this morning, that is. This morning the Queen asked the same old question. But the mirror didn't give her the same old answer. It said:

> *"My lady, you are fair, it's true.*
> *But now Snow White is more fair than you."*

Turn to **page 2.**

2   The Queen flew into a fury when she heard that. She yelled at one of her servants, "Bring the huntsman to me!"

When he came, she said, "I want you to take Snow White deep into the forest. Kill her there. Then cut out her heart and bring it back to me, as a sign that the deed is truly done."

So now you are deep in the forest — and the huntsman is raising his knife.

"Oh, please — please don't kill me," you beg. "Just let me go. Let me run far away."

A look of pity crosses the huntsman's face. "All right, Snow White — go," he says gruffly. "I will kill some wild animal and take its heart to the Queen instead."

So you run away through the woods. Bramble bushes tear at your legs. Tree branches tangle in your hair. Again and again you stumble over roots and stones. Again and again you see wild animals watching you.

Go on to the next page.

But still you keep running. At last you come to a clearing in the woods. In the middle of it is a little house. You peer through a window and see a small table. Around the table are seven small chairs. On the table are seven bowls and seven cups and seven plates. At the far end of the room are seven small beds.

You stare at those beds. How good it would be to lie down for just a little while, you think. But you know you are still not very far from the palace. Should you put more distance between you and your wicked stepmother before you stop to rest?

If you push open the door, turn to **page 30.**

If you force yourself to keep on going, turn to **page 24.**

Your stepmother makes a very good statue. There's that look of hate on her face, of course. But for the very first time you can remember, she is completely silent.

A few days later your father comes home. He sees that look of hate, and the knife in the upraised hand. And then . . . then he knows what his wife is really like.

"But what shall we do with the statue?" he asks. "I don't think we want it here in the palace."

You agree. Finally the two of you decide to take it down to the far, far end of the garden. You place it between two thorn bushes. And then you put a very strong iron cage over it — just in case.

THE END

You don't want the peddler woman to comb your hair. "No, thank you," you say. "I really must go now."

The old woman turns away angrily. As she does, she drops the comb on the ground. There's a sizzling noise, and the grass instantly dies.

So now you know that the old woman is really your wicked stepmother in disguise. When the dwarfs come home you tell them what happened.

"I have to leave here," you say. "She will be back, I know it. So I have to go a lot farther away." The dwarfs are very sad that you're going. But they know you're right.

As you're about to leave, they give you a tiny gold bell. "If you are ever in trouble, ring it three times. Remember, now."

"I'll remember," you promise. Then you kiss each of them and start off through the forest.

You walk for many hours. For a long time you see nothing except trees. But then the trees begin to thin out, and you see a tall cliff ahead. There's a cave at the bottom of it — a cave with smoke coming from it.

Turn to **page 6.**

6   Is someone cooking in there? you wonder. You call, "Hello?" This turns out to be a mistake, for a moment later a fire-breathing dragon comes charging out!

He paws the ground. Then he roars and starts toward you. The look in his eye is easy to read. You are about to become his mid-afternoon snack.

If you remember the little gold bell and ring it three times, turn to **page 28.**

If you're so afraid you forget the bell, turn to **page 39.**

"No, thank you," you say to the King. You know that this young man is no Count at all. And you don't want to be known as his sister when the King finds that out.

So you go on your way. Before long you come to a high hedge — a hedge thick with thorns. Standing in front of it is a worried-looking young man.

"Hello," he says.

Soon the two of you are talking. Peter — for that is his name — tells you that he works for a Prince from a faraway land.

"What are you doing here?" you ask.

"That's what I'm wondering myself," Peter answers. "I think I'm being part of a wild-goose chase."

You look puzzled. Peter tries to explain. It seems that his Prince is on a quest — he's searching for a Princess who is asleep.

"Asleep?" you say. "In the middle of the day?"

"Yes," Peter replies. "It seems that this Princess has been asleep for a hundred years. And only one thing can wake her — the kiss of the right Prince."

Turn to **page 8.**

"And your Prince thinks he's it."

"Right," says Peter. "Half an hour ago we came to this hedge of thorns. He told me to wait. Then he somehow got through the hedge, and I haven't seen him since."

"Don't you want to know what's in there?" you ask.

"Not much," answers Peter. "Do you?"

If you do, turn to **page 55.**

If those thorns look a little too sharp, and you think you've had enough adventure for one day, turn to **page 44.**

You don't want anything to do with that apple. **9**
"Thank you, but I'm not hungry right now," you tell the old woman.

You know who she is, of course. She looks different from the last time she came. But nothing can hide that hateful look in your stepmother's eyes.

How does she know I'm here? you wonder. Then you realize — it's the magic mirror. It's been telling her. Unless you do something about the mirror, you'll never be able to get away from her. Not anywhere.

The old woman has just started off. You call after her, "Oh, don't go away. Wouldn't you like a drink of water? It's so warm today."

"A drink of water?"

"Yes," you say. "Won't you come inside?"

She looks a little puzzled, but she comes in.

"I just have to get the water," you tell her. "I'm keeping it cool down in the cellar."

You open the cellar door and go down a couple of steps. Then you start shouting, "Help! Help! Oh, help me, please!"

At first you don't think she's going to come. So you shout again, "Help! I'm dying, I'm dying!"

Turn to **page 10.**

10   That should get her, you think. She certainly wants to see me dead. And you're right — the old woman comes running. She runs right past you — all the way down the cellar stairs.

But you are hiding behind the door. Now you run back up the steps and into the room. You slam the door behind you and lock it.

Your stepmother starts to pound on the door. But she can't get out, whatever she does.

It's time to take care of that mirror. You start off for the palace. When you get there you slip in through a side door and head straight for your stepmother's room.

You've never been inside it before. As you open the door, you see that the room is alive with strange creatures. Beady-eyed bats hang from the ceiling. Giant spiders wave their hairy arms at you. Snakes glide slowly across the floor. Rats scurry under chairs and peer out at you.

Then you hear a horrible sound. All these creatures are whispering — whispering a warning just for you.

Turn to **page 12.**

"Turn back, Snow White — don't
come too near,
For only death awaits you here."

But you must enter that room. You must! And, your heart pounding, you do. The animals don't attack you — they only go on whispering their warning. You look all around, but the mirror isn't there. Not anywhere.

At last you see a second door. You open it and find another very small room. A skeleton hangs in one corner. A row of skulls grins at you from a shelf. And there on the far wall is her magic mirror.

If you go in and try to smash the mirror, turn
to **page 32.**

If you decide not to smash it because its
powers might somehow be turned to good use,
turn to **page 49.**

You meet the younger brother. The two of you stroll in the palace gardens and talk. At last he stops and sits down. You sit beside him.

"I'm very happy you've come here," he says. "Happier than you can ever imagine."

You look at him, puzzled.

"You see," he goes on, "years ago my fairy godmother told me that one day I must go on a long, long journey. I must search the world until I found a glass coffin on a hill. Inside that coffin would be a beautiful Princess under a spell. I would wake her with a kiss, and she would become my wife."

You still don't understand.

"But now," he says, "you've come here. You've saved me that long boring journey."

"I did?"

"You did," he says. "So you really haven't any choice. You'll have to become my wife — just as my fairy godmother said."

You look at him for a moment. Then you smile. "Well, if *she* said so, then I suppose I'll have to, won't I?"

THE END

14   You get in the coach. So does the young man who is now calling himself the Count of Carabas. He sits next to the Princess, and soon they are talking and laughing. It's plain that they like each other.

You sit beside the King and chat with him. Before long he asks, "Won't you come back with me and meet my son, the Prince? I'm sure you two would be great friends."

If you want to do that, turn to **page 71.**

If you really don't feel like meeting anyone else today, turn to **page 43.**

You know just the kind of help you need. The **15** Queen has magic powers, so you go to someone else who deals in magic, too. He's Marlan, the Court Magician.

You find him in his laboratory, hunched over a bubbling brew. "What can I do for you?" he asks.

You tell him about what's happened to you. Also what is going to happen next if you don't get some help fast.

Turn to **page 16.**

16   Marlan nods his head. "Of course I'll help you, dear child," he says. "I never could stand that woman. Dabbling in things that are none of her business. . . ."

"What can you do?"

"No, no, not I," he answers. "*You* must be the one to challenge her — for you are the one she wants to harm.

"I'm not strong enough."

"Ah," says Marlan, "but I will give you a special magic." He touches your forehead with his finger. He makes three circles over your head. He mumbles something that sounds like, "Slava, klava, molten lava." Then he touches your forehead again.

"There!" he says. "Now all you have to do is point your finger, and whatever you wish will come true."

You thank him and go hunting for your stepmother. It isn't hard to find her. She's screaming, "Where is she? Where is Snow White?"

Go on to the next page.

When she sees you, she screams even louder,
"Now I've got you!!" You see that she has a knife
in her hand.

Quickly you point your finger at her and make
a wish.

If you want her to turn into a statue, turn to
page 4.

*If you want the knife to become a wisp of
straw, turn to* **page 66.**

18   You set out for the palace. When you get there, you slip in through a side door and creep down a long hallway. Then another.

It's very quiet. Much quieter than usual. This puzzles you. At last you notice that all the statues that line the hallways are draped in black cloth.

Why? you wonder. Then suddenly you know. Everyone thinks you are dead. The palace is in mourning for you!

Finally you get to your bedroom. Your faithful maid is there, crying. "Hello, Belinda," you say softly.

She whirls around and lets out a yelp of surprise. "Snow White! You're alive! How can it be?"

"Shhhhhh," you whisper. As quickly as you can, you tell her what happened to you. "So you see, I must speak to my father right away. Can you find him and bring him here?"

Go on to the next page.

Belinda shakes her head sadly. "Oh, Snow White, I can't. He isn't here. When he heard that you died in the forest, he said he couldn't stay where so much reminded him of you. So he rode off with a few of his men. He won't be back for at least three days."

What can you do now?

If you decide to hide in the palace until the King comes home again, turn to **page 58.**

If you think this is too risky, and you'd better get help right away to fight your stepmother, *turn to* **page 15.**

20 "Thank you for asking me to stay," you tell the dwarfs, "but I really must leave. You see, there's something I have to do."

"What's that?" ask the dwarfs.

"I see now that I must go back to the palace and tell my father what has happened."

"Do you think that's wise? Your stepmother is there, too, after all."

"I know. But my father is the King. He will protect me when he knows the truth."

"I hope you're right," the dwarfs say.

So you set out for the palace. When you get there, you slip in through a side door. You creep down a long hallway. And then another.

It's very quiet. Much quieter than usual. This puzzles you. At last you notice that all the statues that line the hallways are draped in black cloth.

Why? you wonder. Then suddenly you know. Everyone thinks you are dead. The palace is in mourning for you!

Turn to **page 22.**

Suddenly, up ahead, the huntsman comes around a corner. You flatten yourself behind a statue as he passes by. A few minutes later, you almost bump into your stepmother. This time you manage to crawl under a big chair. But you needn't have worried. She's too busy muttering strange curses to notice you.

Finally you get to your bedroom. Your faithful maid is there, crying. "Hello, Belinda," you say softly.

She whirls around and lets out a yelp of surprise. "Snow White! You're alive! How can it be?"

"Shhhhhh," you whisper. As quickly as you can, you tell her what happened to you. "So you see, I must speak to my father right away. Can you find him and bring him here?"

Go on to the next page.

Belinda shakes her head sadly. "Oh, Snow
White, I can't. When he heard that you died in
the forest, he said he couldn't stay here where so
much reminded him of you. So he rode off with a
few of his men. He won't be back for at least three
days."

What can you do now?

*If you decide to hide in the palace until the
King comes home again, turn to* **page 58.**

*If you think this is too risky, and you'd better
get help right away to fight your stepmother,
turn to* **page 15.**

You walk on through the woods for hours. At last the trees begin to thin out, and you see light ahead. You must be coming to the end of the forest. You decide to sit down and rest for a little while.

Soon you begin to hear voices. They're coming from somewhere behind you. "Now take off your clothes," someone says in a high, clear voice.

"My clothes?" the other voice asks. It sounds like a young man.

"Yes, all of them. And get in the river."

"Why?"

"Trust me, master," the high, clear voice says. "Leave the thinking to me, and you will soon be rich."

"It sure is a strange way to get rich," the young man's voice answers.

After a little while you get up and peer around a tree. There's a river there, and a handsome young man is swimming in it. Sitting on the bank is a cat — a cat wearing a very fancy pair of high leather boots.

Then the cat looks up and sees you. "Why, hello," he says. "My name's Puss — what's yours?"

"Snow White," you tell him.

Go on to the next page.

"Snow White. That's a nice name. Why don't you come and talk with us for a while?"

The cat and the young man seem friendly enough. And you don't have anywhere special to go. So you sit down for a chat. You and Puss do most of the talking. The young man spends most of his time paddling back and forth, looking unhappy.

Suddenly Puss holds up a paw. "This is it," he says softly. "Keep swimming, master!"

Turn to **page 26.**

26　　Then you hear the sound of a coach. Soon it sweeps into view. It's a King's coach — you can tell by the royal seal on the side. It's not your father's, though.

So you must be in the neighboring Kingdom. You've heard that the King here is a very kind sort of man. You can see him inside the coach, with a beautiful young Princess next to him.

Now Puss jumps up and begins to shout, "Help! My master's drowning! The Count of Carabas is drowning!"

The coach stops, and the King sends two of his men to help the young man out of the water.

"What happened, Puss?" the King asks your new friend the cat.

"Two men stole my master's clothes. I chased them, but they were too fast for me."

"That will never do," says the King. He tells one of his servants to go back to the palace. "Bring me one of my very best suits for the Count of Carabas."

The servant soon returns with a fine suit of clothes, and the young man puts it on. The beautiful Princess peeks out of the coach.

"Ah, my dear," says the King. "Let me introduce you to the Count of Carabas. And this is his cat."

Go on to the next page.

Then the King turns to you. "And who might you be, my dear?"

Before you can say a word, Puss tells him, "This is the Count's sister."

"Very nice to meet you, Countess," says the King. "Won't you and your brother come for a ride with us? There's plenty of room."

If this sounds like a good idea, turn to **page 14.**

If you decide you'd rather not, turn to **page 7.**

You ring the bell as hard as you can. At the last note, a very large knight on a very large horse comes charging out of the woods. He's in full armor.

"Begone, I say!" he shouts at the dragon. Then with one stroke of his sword he slays it.

"Kind sir, you have saved me," you say. "May I ask who you are?"

He takes off the head-piece of his armor, and you cry out in surprise. For it's your father, the King! He leans down and hugs you.

Then your father looks at the dead dragon. "Snow White!" he says suddenly. "Look at that dragon. It's wearing a gold necklace!"

You look, and he's right. But how can that be? A gold necklace on a *dragon*?

Your father says, "I know that necklace — know it well. I gave it to my wife just last year. Snow White, this . . . this is your stepmother."

Go on to the next page.

Your father shakes his head sadly, because now he knows just what kind of a woman she really was. Then he helps you up onto his horse, and the two of you start back toward the palace.

As you come in sight of it, the little gold bell slips out of your hand. It falls to the ground. But that's all right. For you have come to **THE END** of all the trouble it was meant to help you with.

You go into the little cottage. And there are those seven beds. I'm so tired, you think. Maybe I'll lie down for a few minutes.

The next thing you know, it is morning. You open your eyes. And standing around your bed are seven dwarfs, all staring at you.

For a moment, you're scared. But then you notice the look on their faces. They're smiling, all of them. So you say, "Hello."

"Hello," one of the dwarfs answers. "Who are you?"

"My name is Snow White," you say. "And I want to thank you for letting me sleep here all night."

Go on to the next page.

"You're very welcome. But why are you here?"

You tell them about your wicked stepmother and everything that happened yesterday in the woods. "And now I think I should say good-bye and go on my way," you say.

The dwarfs look at each other. "Would you like to stay here? You could help us cook and clean."

*If you think this is a good idea,
turn to* **page 63.**

*If you decide it's too dangerous to stay any
longer, turn to* **page 20.**

32   You take one of the skulls from the shelf and hit the mirror. It shatters into thousands and thousands of pieces.

And then something very strange happens. Those pieces of glass don't fall to the floor — they all go flying through the window. You peer out and see that they are swirling around and around, like a tornado.

Then they begin to come together. They're forming into. . . . Why, they're forming into a coach! That's it — a coach and a team of horses, all made of glass. The door of the coach is standing open.

Somehow you know you're expected to get in. So you go downstairs and out into the courtyard. Once you climb into the coach, it starts off.

Go on to the next page.

At first you don't know where you're going. But then you begin to see things you remember — a river, a tree that's been hit by lightning, a mountain with a double peak. So you're not really surprised when the coach finally pulls to a stop in front of the seven dwarfs' house.

They dash out to greet you. "Come in! Come in!" they say. "We're so glad to see you! We were afraid you got lost."

"No," you tell them. "I just had something to do, back at the palace."

"Well, guess who we've got here. It's your stepmother!"

"I know. I locked her in the cellar."

"Oh, that's how she got there," the dwarfs say. "Anyhow, she wants to stay and work for us — making beds and washing dishes."

Now this *is* hard to believe. "My stepmother wants to do *that?* Why?"

Turn to **page 34.**

"She says something happened back at the palace — something that took away all her magic powers. From now on she will be nothing but an ugly old woman. She doesn't want to go back to the palace looking like that."

Now you understand. *You* know what happened back at the palace, because you did it.

So your stepmother stays in the little cottage, working for the dwarfs. And you? You say good-bye to your small friends and go back to the palace in your glass coach.

And with no stepmother around, you and your father live happily ever after.

THE END

The comb touches your hair. After that, you remember nothing at all. So of course you don't hear the wicked Queen cry, "There! What good is all your beauty now?" as she scurries away.

That evening the dwarfs come home and find you lying on the floor. "She's dead! Snow White is dead!" one of them cries. But then he sees the comb in your hair and pulls it out. Right away you begin to stir. Soon you are sitting up.

"What happened?" the dwarfs ask you.

You tell them about the old woman and the comb.

"The comb must be poisoned," they say. "And that old woman is the Queen in disguise."

"Oh!" you say. "I never would have guessed, to look at her."

The dwarfs warn you again. "Snow White, you must promise never, ever to open the door to anyone. From now on you will be in even more danger."

They are right. The next day you are making beds when you hear a voice outside singing, "Apples for sale! Juicy, ripe apples for sale!"

You remember the dwarfs' warning. So you try not to pay any attention and hope the woman will go away.

Turn to **page 36.**

36   But she doesn't. Finally you peek through the window and see a little old farmer's wife with a basket of bright, shiny apples. How good they look, you think.

The dwarfs made you promise not to open the door. But they didn't say anything about the window. So you open it just a little.

"Please go," you say. "I can't let anyone in."

"Oh, I don't want to come in, dearie," answers the farmer's wife. "All I want is to give you one of my apples." And she holds one out. It's a very beautiful apple, half red and half white.

"It looks very nice," you say politely. "But I can't take it."

"What's the matter, dearie?" the old woman asks. "Why are you so frightened? Look, I'll cut the apple in two. You eat half and I'll eat half. So there's nothing to be afraid of."

Quickly the old woman cuts the apple in half. She takes a big bite out of the white side. Then she holds out the red half to you.

If you take a bite of it, turn to **page 45.**

If you are afraid, turn to **page 9.**

38   You tell the Prince you'll go with him, and he leads you through the hedge of thorns. Outside, his royal coach is waiting. He helps you into it, and soon you are rolling down the road toward his palace.

A moment later you look out the window and see an old woman. Her face is wrinkled. Her hair is white. She's dressed in rags. But you recognize her all the same — it's your stepmother.

She sees you and starts to run after the coach. But she's no match for the four fast horses pulling it. The last you see of her, she's jumping up and down and shaking her fist at you. She's surrounded by a large cloud of dust.

Most of it seems to be settling on her.

THE END

You run away from the dragon. You run faster than you've ever run before. But it's right behind you.

You come to a forest. The trees are very close together, and they slow the dragon down a little. But he's a lot stronger than you are. He just keeps coming. And you're tiring fast.

I can't go on much longer, you think. I can't. I'll have to stop, and that will be the end of everything. But then you come to a small clearing. Lying in the middle of it is a young man, fast asleep.

"Wake up! Wake up!" you shout. "There's a dragon!" But the young man sleeps on. You shake him and scream into his ear. But nothing wakes him. Then you know that he must be under some kind of spell. And the dragon is getting closer by the second.

Turn to **page 40.**

At last you remember the tiny gold bell. You ring it three times. As the last note fades away, the young man opens his eyes and looks up.

The first thing he sees is the charging dragon. He leaps to his feet and draws his sword. The two of them circle each other. The young man lunges forward. The dragon beats him back with a blast of its fiery breath.

Then you get an idea. You creep quietly around behind the dragon. You find a big rock — so big you can hardly lift it. And you drop it on the dragon's tail.

The dragon howls. He turns to lash out at you. At that moment the young man's sword flashes. And that is the end of the dragon.

Once the two of you catch your breath, you sit down and begin to talk. His name, he says, is Prince Michael. Before long you find you have all sorts of things in common.

"How good it is to meet a Princess with something interesting to say," Michael tells you. A while later he asks you, "Why don't you come home with me and be my wife? I'm sure we will never run out of things to say to each other?"

Go on to the next page.

You're sure of this, too. But you shake your **41**
head. "I like you very much," you say, "but I
can't marry you."

"Why not?"

"It's because of who you are."

"Who I am?" Prince Michael doesn't understand.

"Yes — because you're a Prince."

You see that he still doesn't understand. So you
try to explain. "I'm tired of being a Princess. I'm
tired of living in a big palace. I'm tired of wearing
beautiful dresses and riding around in fancy gold
coaches. I'm tired of having people bow down to
me all the time."

"I see," says Prince Michael.

"I only spent a short time at the dwarfs' house,"
you go on. "But I learned something very important
there. The simple life is the one I want. So I'm
afraid I can't marry a prince."

Prince Michael grins at you. "That's no problem
at all," he says, "because I rule over the smallest
Kingdom in the whole world."

"How small?" you ask.

Turn to **page 42.**

"Well, really just a cottage and a side yard."

"Oh," you say. "A large side yard?"

"No, just big enough for a garden and one apple tree," he answers.

"And no servants?"

"Not a one. So you can see I have very little to offer you — except my love."

You smile at Prince Michael. That sounds just about right to you.

THE END

Suddenly, you're feeling very, very tired. You don't want to talk any more, or meet any more new people. You just want to be by yourself.

So the King stops the coach and you climb out. You know exactly where you want to go. It's that little cottage you passed by yesterday. You remember how snug it looked in the middle of that clearing in the woods. You remember peering in the window and seeing seven little chairs around a table — a table that was set with seven little plates, and seven little bowls, and seven little cups. At the far end of the room were seven little beds.

It all looked so friendly, you think. I'd like to go back there.

To go back to the cottage, turn to **page 30.**

"No, I don't think I want to know what's in there, either," you say. "Well, good-bye, now — I'll be on my way." You turn to go.

"Please wait," says Peter. You stop and look at him. "Would you like to meet this Prince's brother?"

"His brother?" you ask, puzzled. "Why should I meet his brother and not him?"

"Well, this Prince is a little strange, I'm afraid. Look at what he's doing now. Chasing off after a Princess he's never even seen — who also happens to be 115 years old."

"You're right. That is a little strange."

"But his brother — now *there's* a real man. He's smart and kind and very handsome. There's only one little thing wrong with him."

"What's that?" you ask.

"He's the younger brother. So he'll probably never become King. But would you like to meet him anyway?"

If you're tired of Princes — younger brother or not — turn to **page 65.**

If you think this brother sounds interesting, turn to **page 13.**

The apple touches your lips. After that you remember nothing at all. Your stepmother poisoned your half of the apple.

That evening the dwarfs come home and find you lying on the floor once more. But this time there is nothing they can do. For three days they sit in a circle around you. Sometimes they cry. Sometimes they talk quietly about what a wonderful person you were.

On the third day, one of them says, "Brothers, it is time to bury Snow White." But the others shake their heads. They can't bear the thought of putting you in the cold, dark ground.

So they build a glass coffin for you. On it they paint SNOW WHITE in gold letters. And under your name they put the word PRINCESS. Then they carry the coffin to the top of a hill.

The dwarfs take turns sitting beside your coffin. The wild animals and birds of the woods come to mourn for you, too.

For a long time you lie there in your coffin on the hill. Then one morning a Prince happens by. "How beautiful she is," he cries when he sees you. "I must have her for my own."

Turn to **page 46.**

He turns to the dwarfs. "Please let me have her," he begs. "I'll give you anything you want."

At first the dwarfs shake their heads. "We wouldn't sell Snow White for all the gold in the world," they say.

But soon they see that the Prince loves you truly. So they take pity on him. "You may take her," they say.

The Prince tells his men to lift up your coffin and carry it on their shoulders. "Be careful," he says. And the men try their best. But then they stumble over a rock in the path.

Go on to the next page.

And that's enough. The coffin is jolted, and the piece of poisoned apple pops out of your mouth. You begin to stir. You raise the glass lid and rub your eyes. "Where am I?" you ask sleepily.

"Oh, my dear," cries the Prince joyfully. "You are alive!"

You look up and see a very handsome young man. "But I don't understand," you say to him. "The last thing I remember is taking a bite out of an apple."

The Prince begins to tell you all that has happened. By the time he is done, the two of you are holding hands.

Turn to **page 48.**

48   "I love you, Snow White," says the Prince. "Will you come and be my wife?"

"I will," you answer. And the two of you ride off together to the Prince's palace.

Before long your wedding is announced. Invitations go out to many important people. One of them is your stepmother, the Queen.

As the wedding is about to begin, she sees you. First she turns white with shock. Then she turns red with rage. Finally she becomes so furious that her heart stops beating. And that's the end of the wicked Queen.

But this is not **THE END** for you. It's just the beginning of a long and very happy life.

You don't have to say anything. The mirror
already knows you're not going to hurt it. It says
softly:

> *"Thank you, thank you, fair Snow White;*
> *Your heart is kind and true,*
> *And so, my dear, it's only right*
> *That I should now help you."*

"*Can* you help me?" you cry. "Oh, please! I
need help so badly."

> *"I first must tell you this, my dear:*
> *The Queen has broken free,*
> *And very quickly will be here;*
> *You must work speedily."*

"But how?" you ask. "Can you tell me what I
should do?"

> *"On yonder shelf beside the door,*
> *You'll find a weighty book;*
> *On page one hundred thirty-four,*
> *Is where you ought to look."*

You find the book. It's called *Spells and Charms*.
You flip through to page 134, and your heart
sinks. There are dozens of different spells and
charms, just on that one page.

Turn to **page 50.**

You start to read. First is a spell that will take hay from someone else's field and put it in yours. No, that's no help. The mirror speaks again.

"Hurry, hurry, Snow White, dear;
The wicked Queen is getting near."

You try another charm. Draw a picture of your enemy, it says. Then stick pins in it. No, that's not much use, either. And the mirror is beginning to sound panicky.

"Hurry, hurry, Snow White, dear;
The wicked Queen is almost here."

Your time is running out — and still you've found nothing. You hear your stepmother on the stairs. Quickly you read on. You've got to find it. You've got to!

Here's a charm to cure warts. She's just outside the door! A spell for lovers' quarrels. The door is opening! A charm for spoiled milk. No, no, no.

And then you find it! Quickly you say the words over to yourself. You look up as your stepmother enters the room. Her face is twisted with fury. "I thought you'd be here!" she screams. "Now I have you!" And she starts forward.

Go on to the next page.

You point three fingers at her. Blinking your eyes three times, you say:

> *"Beelzebub, begone, begone,*
> *You now are banished hereupon,*
> *Nor ever shall you come anon."*

Suddenly your stepmother's face begins to change. The fury fades slowly away. She starts to smile.

Then she holds out her arms. "Oh, Snow White," she says in a loving voice, "I'm so glad to see you. Come, let's find your father. Let's do something wonderful together. I know — let's have a picnic!"

You can hardly believe your ears. You knew it was a good spell. But you didn't know it was *this* good. It must have been, though. For there is your stepmother, suddenly as warm and loving as your own mother was.

Turn to **page 52.**

52   "A picnic?" you say.

"Yes, the best picnic ever. Oh, my dear, we're going to be so happy together, you and I."

As you leave the room, you turn and whisper, "Thank you," to the magic mirror.

And that is **THE END** of your wicked step-mother.

"Thank you, Belinda," you say, "but I have 53 another idea. Go tell my stepmother that you just saw me out by the stables. Tell her she'd better go there at once, or I'll escape."

Belinda does. And your stepmother rushes off. Then you do what you probably should have done to start with — get some expert help.

To do that, turn to **page 15.**

You say good-bye to Peter and walk toward the hedge of thorns. It parts in front of you. A path opens up. You walk through without a scratch.

A moment later you're standing in the courtyard of a great palace. Everywhere you look are people and animals standing as still as statues. All of them fast asleep.

A horse leans against a wall. A row of pigeons sits on a rooftop, their heads tucked under their wings. A stable boy is frozen in mid-step.

Inside the palace things are much the same. The cook is asleep in the kitchen. The butler is asleep in the hall. The King and Queen are asleep on their thrones. There's even a fly asleep on the wall.

But then you hear voices. You follow them until you come to a tower room. And there is the Prince, talking to a young Princess. Or rather, mostly she's talking to him. You stay out of sight and listen.

"La," she says, "how you did startle poor little me."

La? you think. *La?* What does *that* mean?

"I'm sorry," says the Prince.

"Oh, that's all right." The Princess stretches and yawns. "It's time I got up from my nap."

Turn to **page 56.**

Nap? A hundred years is her idea of a nap?

"Now what was I doing before I went to sleep?" She yawns again. "Oh, yes. I was about to take a walk around the garden with some of my ladies-in-waiting. We were going to talk about all the exciting news."

"What sort of news?" the Prince asks. You notice he's beginning to look just a little bored.

"*Well*, you're not going to *believe* this, but Esmeralda has a new dress. And it's *bright red*. Well! I told her I'd jump out a window before *I'd* wear such a thing. It's not only red, but it has *green bows* all over it. Well, everyone *knows* that bows went out *at least* a month ago. . . ."

Just then the Prince catches a glimpse of you peeking into the room. "Hello," he says. "Come in! Come in!"

You do, and he starts chatting with you. He doesn't even look around when the Princess yawns and announces, "You'll excuse me, I'm sure, if I snatch just a tiny bit more beauty sleep."

By then you and the Prince are busy talking about things like books and music and art. That goes on for quite a while.

Go on to the next page.

"It's getting late," he says at last. "And we still have so much to say to each other. Won't you come back to my palace for a visit? I know my mother and father would like to meet you, too."

"But what about her?" You point at the sleeping beauty.

"Oh," says he, "we'll leave her for some other prince. One who's interested in red dresses and green bows. I don't think she'll even remember I was here. But please, won't you come with me?"

If you say yes, turn to **page 38.**

If you're beginning to get just a little tired of talking about books and music and art,
turn to **page 60.**

58   You know just the place to hide. It's a room at the top of a high, high tower. Nobody ever goes there.

On your way to the tower, you see a guard coming down the hallway. There's nowhere to hide, nowhere at all. You grab the black cloth off a statue and drape it over yourself. You stand there holding your breath as the guard goes by. He never gives you a glance.

Once in the tower room, you look around. There's not much here. Just a bed, a chair, and a table. But on the table there's a big, fat book.

You pick it up and read, *Fairy Tales From Around the World.* You turn to the table of contents. "Jack and the Beanstalk," you murmur. "Puss in Boots. Hansel and Gretel. Thumbelina. . . ." You smile happily. All my old favorites, you think. With this, I won't be a bit lonely.

You aren't. Before you know it, two days have passed. Then you hear someone racing up the stairs. The door bursts open. It's Belinda.

Go on to the next page.

"Your stepmother!" she gasps. "The magic mirror has told her you're alive! It said you're hiding somewhere in the palace. She's searching everywhere, and she's coming this way. She's almost at the bottom of the stairs."

"Oh, Belinda, I'm trapped!"

"Maybe not," she says. "What about my hair?"

"Your hair?" you say, looking at her braid. It's coiled around her head.

"You know how long it is," Belinda answers. "I could let it hang out the window. And you could climb down it."

If you accept her kind offer, turn to **page 68.**

If you suddenly think of a different plan, turn to **page 53.**

You say good-bye to the Prince and leave the palace. Outside, you meet Peter. "Are you going?" he says. "Well, I'll walk along with you, if you don't mind."

"What about the Prince?" you ask. "Doesn't he need you?"

"Oh, he'll get along. I'm not really his servant anyhow. I just did this to get away from the palace for a while."

So the two of you go off together. And as you walk you talk. You had a good time with the Prince. But you have a much better time with Peter. He's just plain fun. In fact, he's so much fun that at first you don't see an old lady walking toward you on the road.

But she sees you. And in a flash she comes flying at you. It's your stepmother. And it's plain that she has murder on her mind.

Peter claps his hands three times. Then he says:

"Topsy-turvy, turvy-topsy,
Locust gum and mustard seed,
Case of measles, case of dropsy —
Turn into a prancing steed!"

At that your stepmother becomes a horse.

Go on to the next page.

"I . . . I don't understand," you stammer. "How did you manage *that?*"

"Well, actually," Peter answers, "I'm the Court Magician."

"Court Magician? But you're so young."

"True," says Peter. "I'm still a magician-in-training. And I'll tell you a secret. This is the very first time I've put a spell on anything. But it seemed to work, didn't it? So — how would you like to ride, instead of walk?"

You both look at the horse. It's a very beautiful animal — as beautiful as your stepmother was. But very likely just as mean and tricky as she was, too.

Still, why not ride? So Peter helps you up and you set off. Before long you come to a small house. "This is where I live," says Peter. "Won't you come inside?"

Turn to **page 62.**

62   But first he puts the horse in a barn out back. Then the two of you sit down for a simple meal of bread and cheese and fruit. Before you are finished, Peter has asked you to marry him. And you say yes. For by now you know that you love him very much.

You also love something else — the fact that he's a magician. Your stepmother is still out in that barn, after all. And who can tell if she still has her magic powers? So you'll sleep easier at night knowing that there's someone else around who has magic powers, too.

THE END

"Oh, yes," you say. "I'd like to stay very much." **63**
So after breakfast the dwarfs start off to work, digging for gold in the nearby mountains. But before they leave, they give you a warning.

"Remember," they say, "your stepmother will soon ask the mirror who is the fairest one of all. And it will tell her that you're alive. So don't let anyone in — anyone at all."

"I'll remember," you say.

You spend the day sweeping and dusting and washing. The dwarfs are very bad housekeepers, so there's a lot to do. You are just starting to make dinner when you hear someone cry, "Perfume and belts and fine combs for your hair."

You peek through the window and see an old peddler woman standing outside.

Someone like that can't harm me, you think. So you open the door and look through the things she has brought.

She holds up a bottle of perfume. You shake your head.

"Well, then, what about this?" The old woman shows you a belt made of fine lace. "Just right for your tiny waist."

Turn *to* **page 64.**

Turn to **page 64.**

64   "No," you say. "I think not."

Now she reaches into her sack and pulls out a pretty little comb. "What could be better for taking the tangles out of your hair?" she asks.

"I don't know. . . ."

"Come, come," the old woman says. "Don't be timid. Here, I'll even comb your hair for you."

If you let the peddler woman comb your hair, turn to **page 35.**

If you decide that this probably isn't a very good idea, turn to **page 5.**

"Thank you just the same," you say to Peter.
"But there's something else I have to do right now."

For you're beginning to see that you have handled things the wrong way. You ran away from your wicked stepmother. But if you keep on running, you'll always be scared and always be in danger.

No, there's only one thing you can do to end this fear — that's to fight back.

To do that, turn to **page 18.**

The knife turns to straw — your stepmother drops it with a howl. Then she picks up a heavy stone vase and throws it at you. Again you point your finger. The vase becomes a pillow in midair.

At last she stalks toward you, snarling. It's plain that she's about to strangle you with her bare hands. A third time you point. Your wish is that she be changed into the form that's most like her true character.

There's a puff of smoke . . . a squawk . . . and your stepmother becomes a vulture. Safely locked inside a large iron cage.

Go on to the next page.

Two days later your father comes home and sees the vulture. You tell him what happened. He shakes his head sadly. "But what are we going to do with her? We certainly don't want this awful bird around here for long."

You agree. So you wait until a wild and stormy night. The wind howls. Lightning flashes. Rain beats against the walls. The two of you take the cage up to the palace roof. Then you open the door and watch the vulture fly away.

"Perfect weather for her," your father says. "Now let's go inside and find a nice fire to sit in front of." And that's what you do — happy to know that this is **THE END** of your troubles.

Belinda unpins her hair, and it tumbles out the window. Down, down, down you climb. The tower is very high. But Belinda was right — her hair is very long.

Soon you are safe on the ground. Or are you safe? You look up. And your stepmother is just starting to climb down after you.

But once more Belinda saves you. She loves her long hair. But now she proves that she loves you more. Quickly she grabs a knife and cuts off her braid. Your stepmother plunges to the ground. And that is THE END of her.

When your father comes home, you tell him everything that happened. He's very sad to learn how wicked his wife was. But mostly he's happy that you're alive.

"What can I ever do to make things up to you?" he asks.

"Nothing," you tell him. "Now that I'm out of danger, life is just about perfect."

There is one question you would like answered, though. So one day you go to visit the magic mirror. You say:

"Mirror, mirror, hear my plea;
What does the future hold for me?"

Turn to **page 70.**

70 For a moment the mirror is silent. Then it replies:

> *"Adventure is in store for you,*
> *When a few more months are done;*
> *There's mystery, and danger, too,*
> *And most of all, there's fun."*

"Thank you," you say softly. Who could ask for a happier future than that?

THE END

Once you get to the King's palace, you and the Prince sit in the garden and talk. You soon find that you like many of the same things. You also find that you *dislike* many of the same things.

What you dislike most of all is the job you were both born to — the job of being royal.

"I hate people bowing to me all the time," says the Prince gloomily.

"I hate dressing up all the time," you say, just as gloomily. "And going to all those boring balls."

"And those banquets that go on forever . . ." the Prince says.

"And the parades . . ." you say.

"And having to make all those speeches. . . ."

You nod. "And never being able to do anything for yourself. . . ."

"Yes! That's the worst of all," the Prince agrees. "Always having servants around doing everything for you." Then he sighs. "But what can we do? One day I'll be a King. . . ."

"And I'll probably be a Queen. . . ."

Turn to **page 72.**

72   "You don't have to," a voice says. You both look around. There is Puss.

"What do you mean?" asks the Prince.

"You could resign," suggests Puss.

"Resign?! Resign from being a Prince? Then who would be King when my father dies?"

"What about your sister?" says Puss. "She could become Queen and do the job instead."

You and the Prince look across the garden. There is the Princess and the new Count of Carabas. They are sitting close together on a bench, holding hands and smiling at each other.

"My master doesn't need me anymore," says Puss. "It looks as though he's going to marry the Princess. Then he'll have what he's always wanted — a rich and easy life. So I'm about to leave. Why not come with me?"

"But where are you going?" you ask.

"Who knows?" says Puss. "Wherever my boots take me. But I'll tell you one thing. What I want out of life is to have exciting things happen — at least three a day."

Go on to the next page.

You and the Prince look at each other. You begin to smile. This sounds like what you want, too. So that very afternoon the three of you set off together down the road to adventure — an ex-Princess, an ex-Prince, and a talking cat.

THE END

Did you know that the real story of Snow White and the Seven Dwarfs — the story that has been told for ages — is in this book? If you're not sure which it is, here's how to find it:

Start on **page 1**, go on to **pages 2 and 3**, and when you get to the choice at the end of the page, turn to **page 30**.

Read **pages 30 and 31**, then turn to **page 63**.

Read **pages 63 and 64**, then turn to **page 35**.

Read **pages 35, 36, and 37**, then turn to **page 45**.

Read **pages 45, 46, 47, and 48**.

When you get to "The End" on the bottom of page 48, you've finished the real story of *Snow White and the Seven Dwarfs*.